D1123586

You Are My Best Friend

A long, long time ago, there was a dinosaur who was mean and fierce, nasty and selfish.

TATSUYA MIYANISHI

MUSEYON, New York

"Ha, ha, ha!
Run faster, you weaklings!
If I catch you, I will snap off your horns and bite
your tails!" yelled the Tyrannosaurus,
with his eyes blazing.

"Help!!"

"Ha, ha, ha! What do you mean, 'Help'?
No one is going to help you, fools!
You have to run faster than that,
or I'll catch you. Ha, ha, ha!"

The Styracosauruses ran away as fast as they could.
But then they came to a . . .

CLIFF!

"Ha, ha, ha!
It's all over for you now.
Ha, ha, ha!"

Slowly the Tyrannosaurus walked
toward the Styracosauruses.

The cliff started to crumble.

The Styracosauruses all jumped onto a nearby tree branch.

But the Tyrannosaurus fell . . .

SPLASH!
The Tyrannosaurus fell into the water.
He didn't know how to swim.
Glub, glub, glub. . . .

"Help! Help!"
The Tyrannosaurus sank deeper
into the ocean.

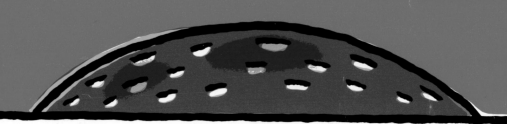

"C-can't swim. C-can't breathe.
Someone, please H E L P!"

But the Tyrannosaurus knew
that he'd been cruel and nasty
and that no one cared about him.

I've done a lot of bad things.
No one will come to help me,
he thought.

Just when he was sure
he was going to die . . .

The Tyrannosaurus landed on a rock.
Slowly his body was lifted up
through the water.

What had seemed to be a rock was
moving upward, carrying him with it.
It went faster and faster,
and then . . .

SPLASH!

The Tyrannosaurus was tossed onto the shore. He landed on his back and was knocked out.

slurp
slurp

When he woke up,
someone was licking his back.

Slurp, slurp, slurp. . . .

"Wh-who are you? Don't eat me!
I won't taste good!" the Tyrannosaurus said.

"Me? Eat you? Oh, no. I'm an Elasmosaurus.
This is going to heal your back quickly.
Slurp, slurp, slurp. . . ."

"Were . . . were you the one who saved
me? Wh-why did you do that?"

"Because you called for help."
The Elasmosaurus smiled.

Looking at the smile on the
Elasmosaurus's face, the
Tyrannosaurus had a strange
feeling inside.

"Th-thank you."
It was the first
time in his life the
Tyrannosaurus had
ever said that.

And as he said it, he
felt a warmth in his
heart.

Then,

"I, I . . . eat meat. Wait—
no, I eat red berries."
The Tyrannosaurus lied
without knowing why.

"Are the red berries tasty?"

"They are. I'll get you some."
Crunch, crunch, crunch. . . .

"Your claws are so big,
and your teeth are so sharp!
You must be very strong."

"Yes, I am."

"That's terrible. I . . . I don't like bullying," the Tyrannosaurus lied again. "I hate the nasty guys who do it!"

"There is a strong creature in the ocean, too. But he is mean and nasty and always bullies weaker dinosaurs," the Elasmosaurus said sadly. "The scar on my back is where he bit me."

"I've heard that you have a very scary bully on the land too. Have you heard of him? He's called the Tyrannosaurus."

The Tyrannosaurus was shocked.

"I . . . I don't know who the Tyrannosaurus is!"

The Elasmosaurus looked into
the Tyrannosaurus's face and said,

"I'm so glad that I met a kind dinosaur
like you. You are so nice!
I'll bet you have lots of friends!"

"Ah, yes. How about you? Any friends?"

"I have . . . no friends."

"Then I will be your friend.
Let's meet here again tomorrow."

The Tyrannosaurus said good-bye
to the Elasmosaurus.

His heart ached as he walked home,
because he'd had to lie in order to
make a friend.

The next day, the Tyrannosaurus and the Elasmosaurus took a walk in the shallow part of the ocean.

The Tyrannosaurus held on to the Elasmosaurus's tail, and he learned a lot about what goes on inside the ocean.

The day after that, the two dinosaurs met again.

This time the Tyrannosaurus showed the Elasmosaurus around the land.

Every day after that,
the Tyrannosaurus
and the Elasmosaurus met.

They became best friends and planned to be together for the rest of their lives.

Together forever and ever. . . .

One day soon afterward,
the Tyrannosaurus went to gather
some red berries for his friend.

The Styracosauruses saw him
and were terrified!

"Run! The Tyrannosaurus
is here!"
"Run awaaay!"

But the Tyrannosaurus
looked different.

He smiled as he picked the red berries.

"Don't worry. As soon as I have enough berries, I'll be on my way."

The Styracosauruses were amazed.

When the Tyrannosaurus had gathered an armful of red berries, he headed toward the ocean.

"ROARRR!"

The Tyrannosaurus shouted in a loud voice, but the Elasmosaurus did not appear.

"WHERE ARE YOU?" the Tyrannosaurus called again.

He held the red berries in his arms and waited for a long, long time.

Finally the sun set and the night fell.

Splash, splash, splash.

The Elasmosaurus slowly moved through the water.

"Hey, buddy, today I got red berries for y— "

But before the Tyrannosaurus could finish,

"H-help . . ."

The Elasmosaurus was trying to come ashore, but he was struggling.

SPLASH!

The Tyrannosaurus waded into the ocean. He didn't think twice. All he wanted to do was to save the Elasmosaurus.

Splash, splash, splash.

Then he dived into the water
and headed to where
the Elasmosaurus was sinking.

The night was silent. Even the ocean
seemed to be still.

SPLASH!

The Tyrannosaurus came up,
holding the Elasmosaurus in his arms.

The Elasmosaurus had bite marks
all over his body.

They had been made by the nasty
dinosaur in the ocean.

"What a terrible thing to do!"

The Tyrannosaurus held the Elasmosaurus tight and carried him back to the shore.

The Elasmosaurus did not move at all.

The Tyrannosaurus cried as he held his friend.

"Nooooo! Nooooo!

"Please open your eyes. You are my only friend. I want to eat red berries with you. . . . Can you hear me?

"I've lied to you. I want to tell you the truth! Th-the true me is mean, nasty, and selfish. I'm really the Tyrannosaurus who everyone hates! I want you to see who I truly am. . . . The true me is—"

But the Elasmosaurus interrupted him.

"T-the true you . . . is kind.
The true you is my friend.
You will always be my friend."

The Tyrannosaurus looked at
his friend, who rested safely in his arms.

"I will take care of you and help you
get better," he said. "And we will be
together forever and ever."

The Elasmosaurus smiled calmly.
"Forever and ever."

YOU ARE MY BEST FRIEND

Kimi Wa Hontouni Sutekidane © 2004 Tatsuya Miyanishi
All rights reserved.

Translation by Mariko Shii Gharbi
English editing by Simone Kaplan

Published in the United States and Canada by:
Museyon Inc.
1177 Avenue of the Americas, 5th Floor
New York, NY 10036

Museyon is a registered trademark.
Visit us online at www.museyon.com

Originally published in Japan in 2004 by POPLAR Publishing Co., Ltd.
English translation rights arranged with POPLAR Publishing Co., Ltd.

Printed in Shenzhen, China

ISBN 978-1-940842-10-3